KATHI APPELT

Merry Christmas, Merry Crow

ILLUSTRATED BY
JON GOODELL

sandpiper

HOUGHTON MIFFLIN HARCOURT　•　Boston　New York

www.hmhbooks.com

The text of this book is set in Truesdell.
The illustrations were painted in oil
and acrylic on canvas.

Designed by Linda Lockowitz

The Library of Congress has catalogued the hardcover
as follows:
Appelt, Kathi, 1954–
 Merry Christmas, merry crow/Kathi Appelt;
illustrated by Jon Goodell.
     p.   cm.
Summary: A busy crow flies around town picking
up all kinds of discarded items and uses them to
create a beautiful Christmas tree.
[1. Crows—Fiction. 2. Christmas trees—Fiction.
3. Stories in rhyme.]
I. Goodell, Jon, ill.   II. Title.
PZ8.3.A554Me   2005
[E]—dc21   2002012641

ISBN 978-0-15-202651-6 hardcover
ISBN 978-0-15-206083-1 paperback

Manufactured in China
LEO 10 9 8 7 6 5 4 3 2 1
4500218152

For Heather Nicole McKay and Kaliska Carey Ross, treasures!
—K.A.

For Kathi, with thanks for the gift of her wonderful words
—J.G.

Wind's a blowin'
Sky's a snowin'
 Where's this feathered
  fellow goin'?

Round the chimneys
Over the yards
Down the busy boulevards

A button here
A feather there
    A crow can find things anywhere!

A strand of tinsel
Twigs and twine
    Berries from a twisty vine

'Cross the plaza
Through the zoo
Along the crowded avenue

A shiny ring

A piece of string

A length of garland glimmering

Colored glass

A bottle cap

Fancy gold and silver wrap

Behind the market
Past the shops

This crow is making all the stops!

A broken chain

A lonely sock

A single key without its lock

Some scraps of cloth
A crimson bow
A perfect sprig
of mistletoe

Hustle, bustle
Coming, going
So much busy
to-and-fro-ing

What's his hurry?
What's his mission?
What's his secret expedition?

A silky flower
A paper star
A misbegotten racing car

Candy wrappers
Red and brown
A treasure lost, a treasure found

Atop the flagpole
'Midst the seats

Up and down the snowy streets

Jangly tags
A tiny wheel
A luscious curl of orange peel

A string of beads
A tinkly bell
What's he doing? Will he tell?

One last stop
A bag of seeds

That's everything this tired crow needs

A flap of wings
A cry of glee—
What a perfect Christmas tree!

A magic sight
All hearts aglow

Merry Christmas, merry crow!